Baby's toys

Fiona Watt

pictures by Rachel Wells

managing designer: Mary Cartwright   series editor: Jenny Tyler

What a lot of toys!

Which one shall I play with?

I love noisy toys...

Here comes the train.

Hello, Bunny. How are you?

Bunny, where are you?

Hugging Bunny is best.

Come on Spotty.

I want to build a tall tower.

Whoops!

Let's hide under the playmat.

Silly Fido's in a tangle.

Let's go for a walk.

Usborne Baby's World

Baby's toys